Bayo

A Good African Boy

Judith Hudson

Dedicated to: all the good boys and girls of the world, especially Casey and Alexis.

Love, Grandma Judy

This is a work of fiction. The events and characters described herein are imaginary and are not intended to refer to specific places or living persons. The opinions expressed in this manuscript are solely the opinions of the author and do not represent the opinions or thoughts of the publisher. The author represents and warrants that s/he either owns or has the legal right to publish all material in this book.

Bayo A Good African Boy
All Rights Reserved.
Copyright © 2009 Judith Hudson
v4.0

Illustrations © 2009 Outskirts Press, Inc. All rights reserved - used with permission.

This book may not be reproduced, transmitted, or stored in whole or in part by any means, including graphic, electronic, or mechanical without the express written consent of the publisher except in the case of brief quotations embodied in critical articles and reviews.

Outskirts Press, Inc.
http://www.outskirtspress.com

ISBN: 978-1-4327-4067-2

Outskirts Press and the "OP" logo are trademarks belonging to Outskirts Press, Inc.

PRINTED IN THE UNITED STATES OF AMERICA

This Book Belongs To:

_____

Near the Serengeti Plains of Tanzania, on the rim of the ancient Ngorangora Crater, by the dusty road leading to the city of Arusha, close to the beaten path through the center of a village, on the north side of the path, in the native hut with its rounded thatched roof, lived Bayo's family.

Bayo was the youngest of the family.
Bayo always came when his mother called.
Bayo carried wood for the family's cooking fire.
Bayo helped his father care for the cows and goats.
Bayo was a very good African boy.

Good boys of the village, like six-year old Bayo, herded the goats to pasture everyday. Good boys could be trusted with the goats. Bayo herded his brown milking goat to the pasture. Bayo kept the brown goat safe every day while it grazed on the rich, savannah grass.

On this day, he and the other boys had taken their families' cows and goats to the pasture early. The animals grazed in the pasture on the Serengeti plains. The Tanzanian sun was very hot. Bayo sat in his favorite spot under a large acacia bush at the edge of the pasture watching his goat eat.

The bright rays from the sun were very warm. The morning was very long. The brown goat ate very slowly. Soon Bayo fell asleep under the bush. He slept and he slept and he slept.

When the noon sun was high in the sky, the other boys herded the cows and goats back to the village. They took Bayo's brown goat with them. They left Bayo sleeping in the soft, warm African breeze under his favorite acacia bush.

A small gecko slithered over Bayo's toe and his eyes snapped open. He looked around. He saw the tall kopje rock mounds but not his friends. He saw the giant baobob tree but not the goats and cows. Where were the other boys? Where was the herd? Where was his brown goat? Bayo's mother and father trusted him with the goat because he was a good boy. Bayo's mother and father would not be happy if he came home without the goat. The precious, brown goat gave milk to drink. The goat was gone and Bayo was all alone. Bayo hung his head in shame.

The low afternoon sun in the sky told Bayo why he was hungry. His mother would be worried. His father would be looking for Bayo and the brown goat. His mother and father would not think he was such a good boy. Bayo decided he would just stay away from the village until after dark. Then, he could creep home and sleep in the cow's hut. Tomorrow his mother and father would be happy to see him. Maybe they would forgive Bayo for losing their brown goat.

All alone, Bayo headed back to the village. He walked and walked in the hot sun. Just outside the village, Bayo passed by a wild fig tree. From this tree, he could see his family's thatched rounded roof hut in the village. The sun blazed down on Bayo's brown shoulders. The sun beat down on Bayo's bare head. The sun glinted in Bayo's eyes. Bayo sat in the shade of the tree's umbrella to rest for just a minute.

Round seedpods were everywhere under the wild fig tree. Bayo rolled some seedpods with his foot. The seedpods were great fun. Bayo drew a circle in the sand. He kicked a seedpod. It rolled into the circle. Bayo's foot tapped another seedpod. This one missed the mark. After ten tries, Bayo had seven seedpods in the circle. He would be the winner if the other boys were here to play. Bayo was all alone to play the game. He was all alone with the shame of losing his family's milking goat.

The hot sun and warm breeze made Bayo's tongue stick to the roof of his mouth. His water bag was empty. Bayo walked to the stream near the wild fig tree. Bayo's foot stepped in a large circle shaped hole, the footprint of the elephant. Bayo's toes stuck in a pointed hole, the hoof print of the zebra or the giraffe. Bayo's hands reached into a rounded hole, the paw print of the lion or the hyena. Wild animals came to the stream to drink at night. Elephants, lions, hyenas, wildebeests, water buck, giraffes, and zebras lived near the stream. Bayo drank from the stream quickly and raced back to his seedpod game under the wild fig tree.

The sky was becoming dark and the twilight made Bayo think of his sleeping platform covered with soft warm blankets. Bayo could smell his favorite stew cooking in the pot over the fire. Bayo saw his mother stir the pot. Bayo's father was walking around the fire to the animal pen with the bucket for milking the cows and goats. Soon Bayo could creep into the cow's hut to sleep for the night on the hard ground.

Screech! He! He! He! He! He! In the gathering dark, Bayo heard the scream of the dangerous wild hyena. It was close. Bayo squeezed his eyes shut and put his hands over his ears. Still, the wild scream echoed in Bayo's ear again, only closer. The hyena came to drink at the stream near this wild fig tree. Hyenas were hunters at night and could kill a small water buck. Could the hyena kill a small African boy? Bayo again heard Screech, He, He, He, He, He! The scream was louder and it was closer.

Trembling, Bayo's eyes opened wider and he saw the light of the cooking fire outside his family's hut. Maybe he even saw the shadow of his mother in the light. Maybe his father would be finished milking the cows and goats by now. He heard the loud screech of the hyena repeat. This time the HE! HE! HE! HE! HE! was much too close.

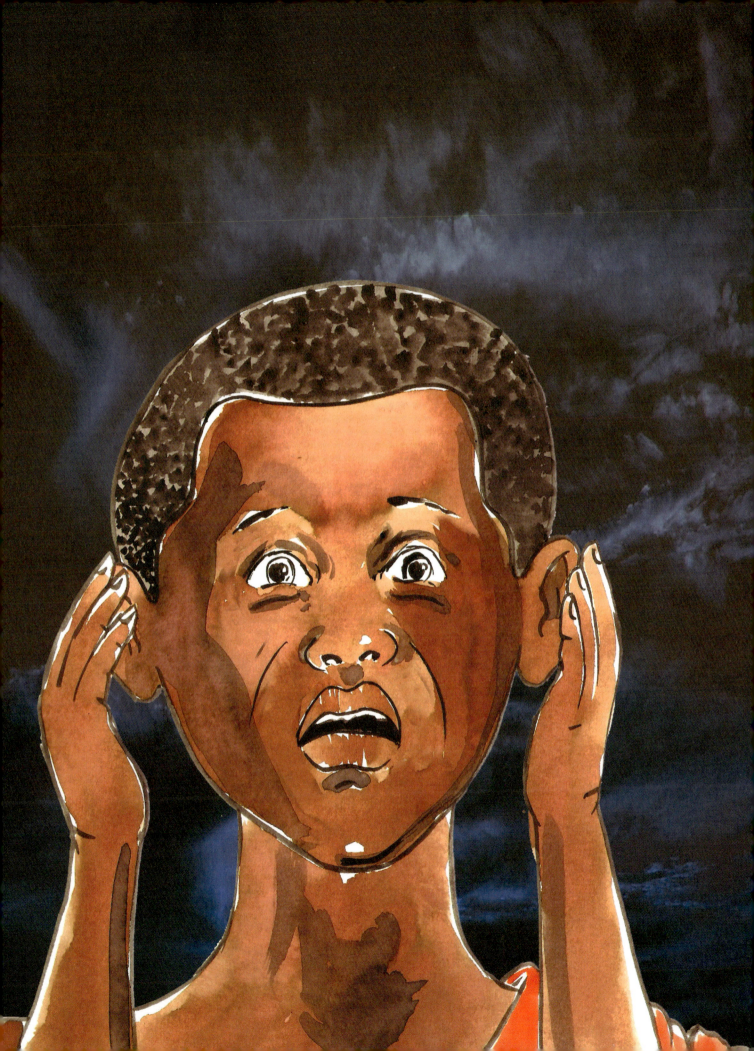

Bayo dashed to the village as fast as his six-year old legs could run. He ran right to his mother's welcoming arms. Over her shoulder, Bayo saw the brown goat tied to the fence. With a tear in his eye, Bayo knew his friends had protected the family's precious, brown goat. Bayo's father handed him the milk bucket as usual. Bayo left his mother's arms to milk the goat as usual. Only Bayo heard a distant Screech, He, He, He, He, in the darkness as milk splashed in the bucket as usual!

The next day before breakfast, Bayo carried water for the cooking pot.
Bayo swept the path to the thatched roof hut for his mother.
Bayo braided a new sisal rope for his father.
Bayo WAS a good African boy.

Then after breakfast, on this day, Bayo untied the brown goat and followed the other boys to the pasture, leaving his native hut on the north side of the path, near the center of a village, close to the dusty road leading to the city of Arusha, on the rim of the Ngorangora Crater, near the Serengeti Plains of Tanzania, Africa.

CPSIA information can be obtained
at www.ICGtesting.com
Printed in the USA
BVIC00n2342021214
377295BV00003B/3